PEANUTS®

SNOOPY®

and Friends

sed on the comic strips by Charles M. Schulz

Popcorn
ELT
Readers

Meet ...
everyone from
PEANUTS
SNOOPY and Friends

Charlie Brown

This is Charlie Brown and these are his friends. Charlie Brown likes helping his friends.

Snoopy

Snoopy is Charlie Brown's dog. He is very clever.

Schroeder

piano

This is Schroeder. He loves his piano.

Lucy

This is Lucy. She loves Schroeder.

kite-eating tree ....o

kite

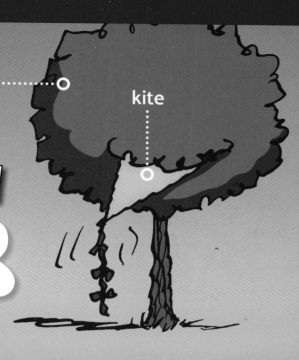

Peppermint Patty

This is Peppermint Patty. She loves to talk but she doesn't like to listen.

Marcie

Marcie is Peppermint Patty's friend.

Before you read ...
What do you think? Does Snoopy help his friends?

New Words

What do these new words mean? Ask your teacher or use your dictionary.

collar

Woof!

The dog is wearing a **collar**.

certificate

Good work! Here is your **certificate**.

expensive

The car is very **expensive**.

climb

She is **climbing**.

hide

They are **hiding**.

learn

They are **learning** to swim.

rescue team

Here comes the **rescue team**!

noisy

It's very **noisy**!

training

This is a **training** school for dancing.

'You're in trouble'

You're in trouble!

poster

She put the animal **poster** in her bedroom.

ANIMALS OF AFRICA

Verbs

Present	Past
fall	fell
think	thought
learn	learnt

PEANUTS®

The KITE-EATING TREE and the Piano

Schroeder loved playing his piano. And Lucy loved Schroeder. But she didn't love his piano.

Lucy was angry. 'You never look at me. You never talk to me. I don't like that piano!'

The next day, Schroeder asked, 'Where's my piano?'

'In a tree,' said Lucy.

'What?' shouted Schroeder. He ran off. He wanted to find it.

Schroeder looked up into the tree. Then he saw Charlie Brown.

'My piano's in this tree,' he said.

'Oh no!' said Charlie Brown. 'This is the kite-eating tree. It eats my kites!'

'Help!' shouted Schroeder. 'This horrible tree is eating my piano. Get the rescue team.'

Snoopy came. He was the rescue team!

'Snoopy can help us,' Charlie Brown said to his friend.

'Dogs can't climb trees!' said Lucy.
'Hmmm...' thought Snoopy.

'Quick, Snoopy!' said Charlie Brown. 'You can climb the tree.'

'He's not a cat!' said Lucy.

Snoopy climbed the tree.

MEOW!

But then … Snoopy fell down.

'Meow,' said Snoopy.

Schroeder was not happy. 'Help me, someone,' he cried.

CHOMP
CHOMP
CHOMP

Charlie Brown looked up into the tree. 'Sorry,' he said. 'This tree's always hungry.'

The next day, Schroeder was very sad.

'My piano, my piano,' he said.

Lucy was angry again. 'You never talk to me,' she said. 'You never look at me.'

'My piano,' said Schroeder.

THE END

PEANUTS®

The Number One
TRAINING SCHOOL

Peppermint Patty wanted to go to a new school.

'New schools are very expensive, Snoopy,' she said. 'What do I do now?'

Snoopy showed her a poster.

'The Number One Training School,' read Patty. 'Twenty-five dollars!'

'Hey, Charlie Brown!' Patty was happy. 'Look at this new school! It's not expensive!'

Charlie Brown looked at the poster. 'Everyone at the school has a dog,' he said. 'Wow!'

He looked at it again. 'But it's a training school,' he said. 'It's a school for ...'

But Patty didn't want to listen. 'This is my new school,' she said. 'Thanks, Snoopy!'

It was Patty's first day at her new school. 'Why do I have this collar?' she thought.

'Do you have a dog?' asked the teacher.
'No, I don't,' she said.

The class was very noisy. And there weren't any tables.

After school, Patty saw her friend, Marcie. 'My new school is great,' she said. 'Today we learnt to sit.'

Then she talked to Charlie Brown. 'My school is great!' she said.

Charlie Brown went to Snoopy. 'You're in trouble!' he said. 'Patty doesn't know it but she's at a school for dogs.'

'Quick! Hide!' thought Snoopy.

Patty learnt a lot!

Soon, Patty had her school certificate.

'Wow!' she said. 'That was quick. No more school for me!'

'Our teacher wants to see your certificate,' said Marcie.

Snoopy went with Patty to her old school. 'Here's my certificate from the Number One Training School,' she said to her teacher.

The teacher looked at the certificate. Snoopy wanted to run away.

'You went to a school for dogs!' the teacher said.

'What?' shouted Patty.

Patty went to Charlie Brown's house. 'Where's your dog?' she said. She was very angry. 'Where is he? Where is he?'

'I don't know,' said Charlie Brown. 'I can't find him.'

THE END

Dog training

All dogs need training! But what do you say and when?

1 *Heel!* When do you say it? If your dog wants to run!

2 *Sit!* When do you say it? If you want to put on your dog's lead.

3 *Drop!* When do you say it? If your dog finds a shoe!

4 Come here!

When do you say it? If your dog is running away!

5 Good boy! / Good girl!

When do you say it? If your dog does 1, 2, 3 or 4.

6 Bad dog! When do you say it? If your dog doesn't do 1, 2, 3, or 4.

★ Do you have a dog? Do you train it? What does it do? ★

What do these words mean? Find out.

need   heel   lead   drop

After you read

1 Snoopy, Schroeder or Lucy? Answer the questions.

Snoopy

Shroeder

Lucy

a) Who is angry? .... Lucy ....

b) Who loves his piano? ....

c) Who is the rescue team? ....

d) Who puts a piano into a tree? ....

e) Who climbs the tree? ....

f) Who loves Schroeder? ....

2 Put the sentences from *The Number One Training School* in order. Write 1–6

a) Peppermint Patty learnt to sit. ☐

b) Snoopy showed Peppermint Patty a poster. ☐1☐

c) Peppermint Patty was very angry. ☐

d) The new school was very noisy. ☐

e) Peppermint Patty went to a new school. ☐

f) Snoopy wanted to run away. ☐

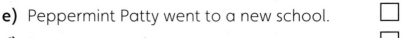

Where's the popcorn?
Look in your book.
Can you find it?

Puzzle time!

1 Who or what is this?

a)

b)

c)

Charlie Brown

....

d)

e)

f)

....

2a Find the dogs and write the numbers.

i) ...**Five**.. dogs are eating.

ii) .... dogs are jumping.

iii) .... dogs are sitting.

iv) .... dogs are hiding.

b How many dogs are there in total? ....

3 Write the words.

a) <u>n</u> <u>o</u> <u>i</u> <u>s</u> <u>y</u>

b) _ _ _ _ _ _ _ _ _ _ _ _

c) _ _ _ _ _ _

d) _ _ _ _ _

4a Who's this? Finish the picture.

b Do you like this character? Why / why not?

....

Imagine ...

Work in pairs. Act out the scenes.

A		
Patty:	Hey, Charlie Brown! Look at this new school! It's not expensive!
Charlie Brown:	Everyone at the school has a dog. Wow! But it's a training school for ...
Patty:	This is my new school. Thanks, Snoopy!

B		
Patty:	Here's my certificate from the Number One Training School.
Teacher:	You went to a school for dogs!
Patty:	What?

Chant

Schroeder's piano

Schroeder's piano is in a tree!
Who put it there?
Lucy!

Lucy put the piano in a tree!
Which tree?
The kite-eating tree!

The piano is in the kite-eating tree!
Who can help?
Snoopy!

2 Say the chant.